FIND THE DINOSAUR

igloobooks

MEET THE DINOSAURS!

Ten little dinosaurs are hiding on every page in this fun book! Read the profiles below to learn all about each of the roar-some creatures. Then, look carefully at the scenes to try and find where they are all hiding. The answers are at the back of the book so you can check your searching skills.

TWINKLE

LOVES:
Ballet dancing

FAVORITE OUTFIT:
Pink tutu

BEST DANCE MOVE:
The twirl-stomp

DOTTY

FAVORITE GAME:
Hide-and-stomp

ALWAYS WEARS:
Cozy sweater

FAVORITE BOOK:
The thesaurus

REX

FAVORITE MEAL:
Afternoon tea-rex

KNOWN FOR:
Tyranno-snoring loudly

ALWAYS WEARS:
Green neckerchief

VIOLET

LOVES:
Prehistoric flowers

PERSONALITY:
Friendly and sweet

FAVORITE COLOR:
Purple

SPIKE

DISLIKES:
Dino-chores

KNOWN FOR:
Can't tricera-stop
telling jokes

ALWAYS WEARS:
Red hat

STEVE

ALWAYS WEARS:
Bowler hat

HOBBY:
Sings in the
tyranno-chorus

LOVES:
Bow ties

TILLY

SECRET TALENT:
Pter-rific at tap dance

HALLOWEEN COSTUME:
Terror-dactyl

MOST-LOVED ACCESSORY:
Star glasses

LEO

KNOWN FOR:
Being super fast

BIGGEST GOAL:
To be a famous velocir-actor

FAVORITE FOOD:
Rock cake

SPOT

FAVORITE THING TO DO:
Shop at dino-stores

MOST-EATEN SNACK:
Volcano ice cream

PERSONALITY:
Always cheerful

DANI

FAVORITE ACCESSORY:
Cozy scarf

SECRET TALENT:
Cave painting

FAVORITE COLOR:
Blue

FOSSIL FUN

There's so much to see at the Dino Museum!
Can you find all ten dinosaur friends?

CAN YOU SPOT THE RED FOSSIL?

JURASSIC JUNGLE

The noisy jungle is full of ROARS and SQUAWKS!
Where are all ten dinos hiding?

CAN YOU SPOT THE YELLOW MUSHROOM?

DINO SPORTS

The dinos love joining the fun at field day!
Can you spot where all ten are hiding?

CAN YOU SPOT THE PURPLE TENNIS BALL?

SEASIDE STOMP

The dinos love sunbathing and splashing in the sea.
All ten are hiding at the seaside. Can you spot where?

CAN YOU SPOT THE YELLOW BIRD?

CANDYLAND CRUNCH

The dinosaurs love to MUNCH and CRUNCH on sweets!
Can you spot all ten dinosaurs in the scene?

CAN YOU SPOT THE PINK COOKIE?

PREHISTORIC PLANET

The dinos love exploring faraway planets! Zoom among the astronauts and aliens to find all ten dinos.

CAN YOU SPOT THE GREEN MOON?

CHOC-OSAURS

The dinos have sneaked into this chocolate factory hoping for a yummy snack! Can you spot all ten?

DINO DISCO

It's party time! This costume party is perfect
for dancing dinos. Can you find all ten?

CAN YOU SPOT THE RED MUSIC NOTE?

TOY-REX TROUBLE

Look at all the toys in this busy shop!
Can you see all ten dinos hiding here, too?

CAN YOU SPOT THE RED GUITAR?

AMAZING ANIMALS

The farmyard is full of noisy animals.
Look closely! There are ten dinosaurs to find.

CAN YOU SPOT THE PURPLE SQUIRREL?

FOSSIL FUN

JURASSIC JUNGLE

DINO SPORTS

SEASIDE STOMP

CANDYLAND CRUNCH

PREHISTORIC PLANET

CHOC-OSAURS

DINO DISCO

TOY-REX TROUBLE

AMAZING ANIMALS

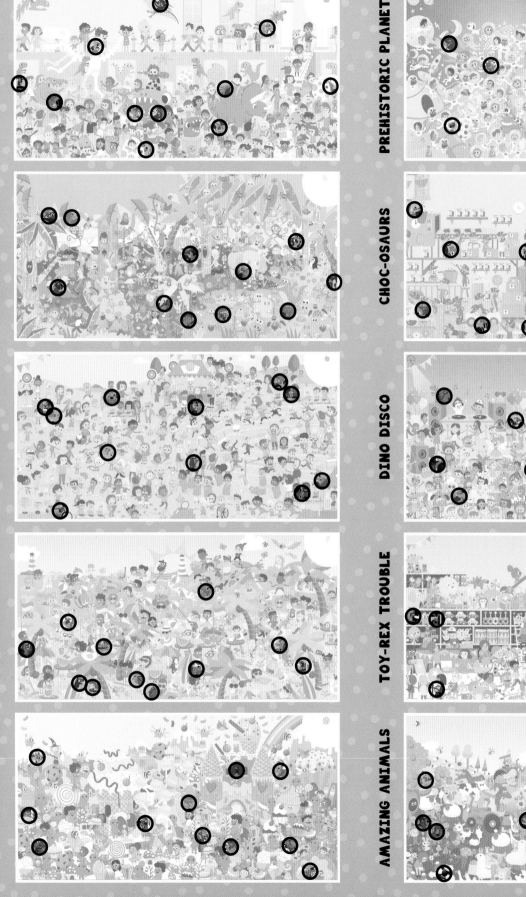
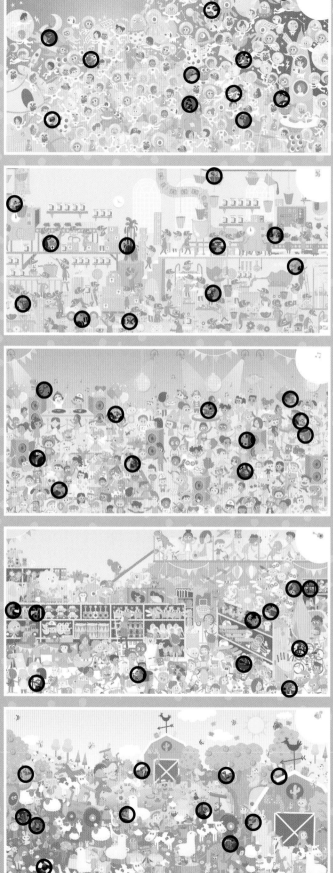